YOU DON'T HAVE TO PET TO BE POPULAR

CARTOONS BY LIBBY REID

PENGUIN BOOKS

PENGUIN BOOKS

PUBLISHED BY THE PENGUIN GROUP

VIKING PENGUIN, A DIVISION OF PENGUIN BOOKS U.S.A. INC., 40 WEST 23RD. STREET, NEW YORK, NEW YORK 10010, U.S.A.
PENGUIN BOOKS LTD, 27 WRIGHTS LANE, LONDON W8 5TZ, ENGLAND
PENGUIN BOOKS AUSTRALIA LTD, RINGWOOD, VICTORIA, AUSTRALIA
PENGUIN BOOKS CANADA LTD, 2801 JOHN STREET, MARKHAM, ONTARIO, CANADA L3R 1B4
PENGUIN BOOKS (N.Z.) LTD, 182-190 WAIRAU ROAD, AUCKLAND 10, NEW ZEALAND

PENGUIN BOOKS LTD, REGISTERED OFFICES: HARMONDSWORTH, MIDDLESEX, ENGLAND

FIRST PUBLISHED IN PENGUIN BOOKS 1989 PUBLISHED SIMULTANEOUSLY IN CANADA
10 9 8 7 6 5 4 3 2 1

MANY OF THE CARTOONS IN THIS BOOK WERE FIRST PUBLISHED AS POSTCARDS OR IN THE WEEKLY CARTOON FEATURE
"CITY WOMAN'S HOME COMPANION" IN THE DAILY NEWS MAGAZINE. "DO YOU KNOW THIS DORM ROOM?" FIRST APPEARED
IN "IN VIEW" AND "LOVE SHOP" APPEARED ON THE RECORD ALBUM COVER FOR CHRISTINE LAVIN'S "ANOTHER WOMAN'S MAN"

LIBRARY OF CONGRESS CATALOGING IN PUBLICATION DATA

REID, LIBBY.
YOU DON'T HAVE TO PET TO BE POPULAR / LIBBY REID.
P.   CM.
ISBN 0 14 011879 9
1. INTERPERSONAL RELATIONS—CARICATURE AND CARTOONS. 2. AMERICAN WIT AND HUMOR, PICTORIAL. I. TITLE
NC1429. R435 A4   1989
741.5'973—DC20   89-3897

PRINTED IN THE UNITED STATES OF AMERICA

for
Janie and Mary
and Mel and Meg

CALLING ALL SPINSTERS!

Are you worried that your lonely, empty, Manless existence is far too happy? Are you considering adding a love-mate to your lifestyle? First you must come to terms with these popular love-squelchers...

What if you are crazy about BIG MUSCLES and Mr. Right looks like this?

Have you considered the sensitive emotions of your Pets?

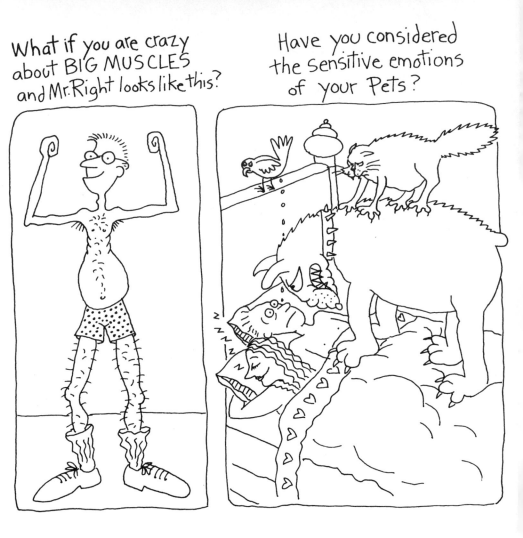

Perhaps L.S.E. World wasn't as much fun to visit as you'd hoped and now you seek a cure for your L.S.E. problem. In a life as bland as yours, major gratificants are elusive. What you need is to begin collecting TINY VICTORIES

3 OUT OF 4 DOCTORS AGREE THAT ON A CELLULAR LEVEL TINY VICTORIES (T.V's) LOOK JUST LIKE HAPPY FACES. THIS DIAGRAM GRAPHICALLY DEPICTS T.V. CELLS DEALING WITH TINY FAILURE (T.F.) CELLS.

Dr. Goodgal

HOW TO BUILD UP YOUR T.V.'s:

☺ MAIL SOMETHING TO A FOREIGN COUNTRY

☺ LEARN TO EAT AN INTIMIDATING VEGETABLE (ARTICHOKE WILL DO)

☺ NEXT TIME SOMEONE STEPS ON YOUR TOES, DON'T SAY, "EXCUSE ME".

REMEMBER! T.V.'s are just as cumulative as T.F.'s. Collect your favorite!

BITTER MAN TEST

T	F	
☐	☐	Take away their cosmetics, high heels and trick clothes and all you have are naked women
☐	☐	Women are money-sucking big-butt crybabies
☐	☐	They are sneaky, squeaky, pea-brained sperm thieves
☐	☐	They're a pack of bossy frigid sluts

YOUR BITTER SCORE: You and an equivalent scorer of the opposite sex will spend a weekend together locked in a tiny, sound-proof rubber room!

The 4 Major Female STRESS PRODUCERS

Pick Your Personal Favorite or Mix 'N' Match 'em!

Ask yourself: Do I always shop with a realistic body image?

Micro-Mini Skirts are for abnormally perfect legs

or Fashion Rogues who don't mind being considered Pitiful Sluts

WHAT'S YOUR FASHION STATEMENT?

CHECK ONE

☐ I'm red hot, yet I command reverential respect

☐ Hey, Sailor, want a date?

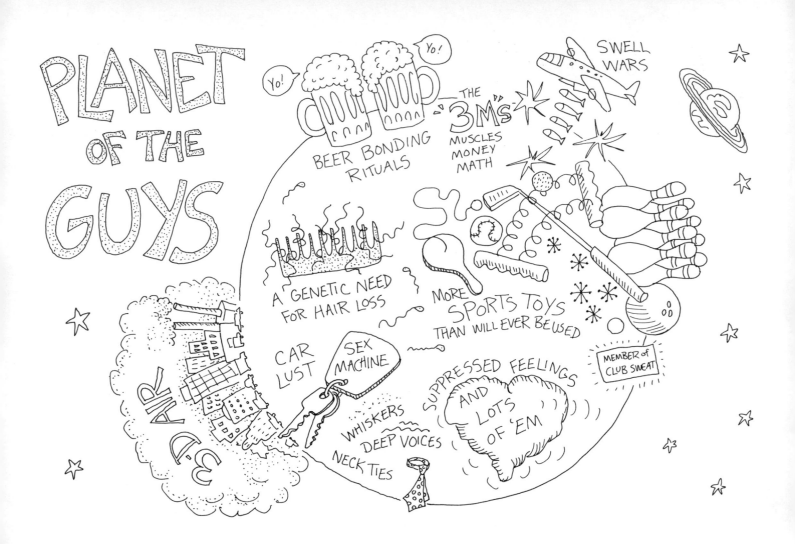

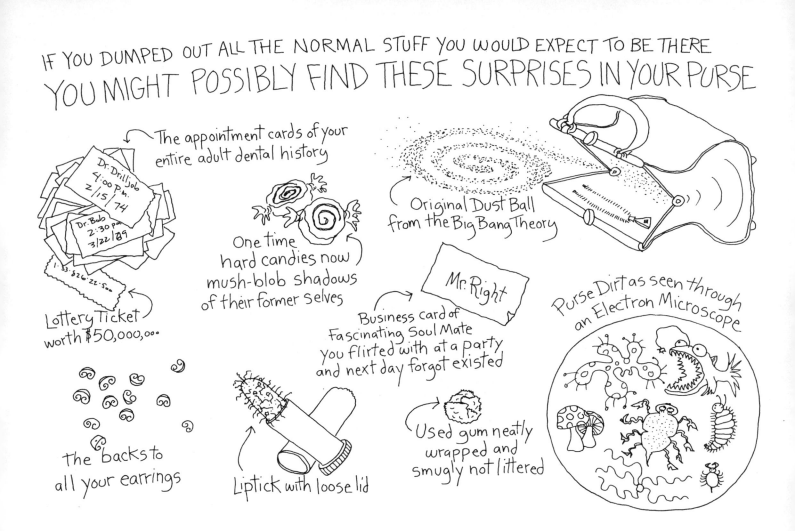

IF YOU DUMPED OUT ALL THE NORMAL STUFF YOU WOULD EXPECT TO BE THERE
YOU MIGHT POSSIBLY FIND THESE SURPRISES IN YOUR PURSE

The appointment cards of your entire adult dental history

Dr. Drilljob
4:00 P.M.
2/15/74

Dr. Bob
2:30 pm
3/22/89

1-33-826-22-5-00

Lottery Ticket worth $50,000,000

One time hard candies now mush-blob shadows of their former selves

Original Dust Ball from the Big Bang Theory

Mr. Right

Business card of Fascinating Soul Mate you flirted with at a party and next day forgot existed

Purse Dirt as seen through an Electron Microscope

the backs to all your earrings

Liptick with loose lid

Used gum neatly wrapped and smugly not littered

User Un-Friendly Kissers
Pucker Up, Baby, You know you love it!
THE FRENCH BANDIT
A.K.A:
· Boss
· Funny Uncle
· Lecherous Old Fart
How about a Friendly Little Kiss for your Old Uncle?
THE DRIBBLE MONGER
I'm 75% Water and Proud of it!
A.K.A:
· Slobber King
· Wet and Wild
· The Liquidator
THE SANDBLASTER
I Hate Shaving - I've got sensitive skin!
A.K.A:
· Kiss'n' Peel
· Weekend War Zone
· Mr. Buff-Puff
ROUGH 'N' READY
Yo! Wanna see me crush a Beer can full of Live Mice with my Lips?
A.K.A:
· Hulking Lummox
· Psycho-Timebomb
· Extra "Y" chromosome
PARTY HEARTY

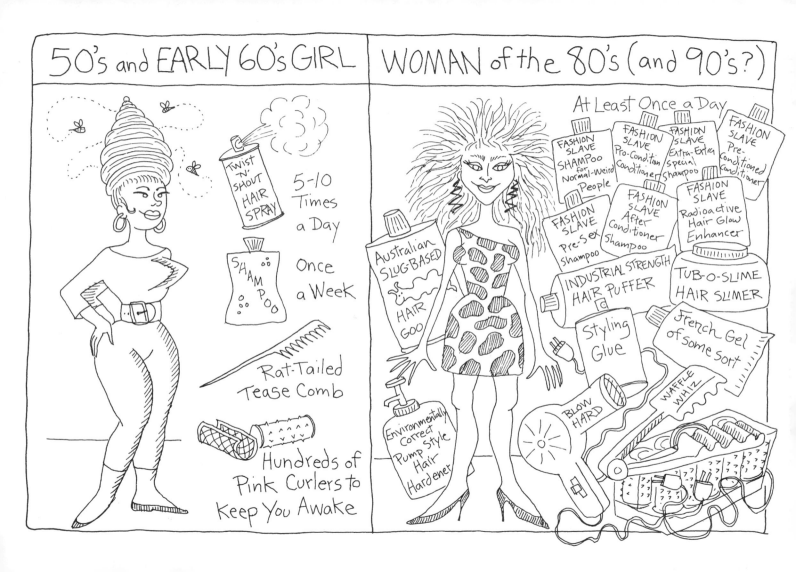

RUNNING OUT OF CUTE YEARS

The unlined Vixen I've known for ages
Is sneaking up on other stages.

I'm Running out of Cute Years!
Whine the ancient ugly fears.

Men will look on me a brand new way
Like at a wall or Great Aunt May.

Even Hoots from passing Sleazes
Soon will be meant for my nieces.

Nature's cruel timing is so unfair
Pimples clear up and Wrinkles appear.

Think you want too much FOOD? Wrong! FOOD WANTS YOU too much. Didn't you know that food gets around by traveling on your hips? Food convinces you to take it home by whispering subliminal come-ons you didn't even know you heard. Listen carefully! Buyer Beware!

CELIBACY! It's not just for Pontiffs, Geeks and Zealots anymore! Creepy modern problems have forced hordes of sexy single people to blunder into the World of Celibacy. Their once frisky sex cells, all dressed up with no place to go, run screaming through their unrequited bodies and rise like hot air, causing unpleasant brain problems.

This is what happens. ⟹

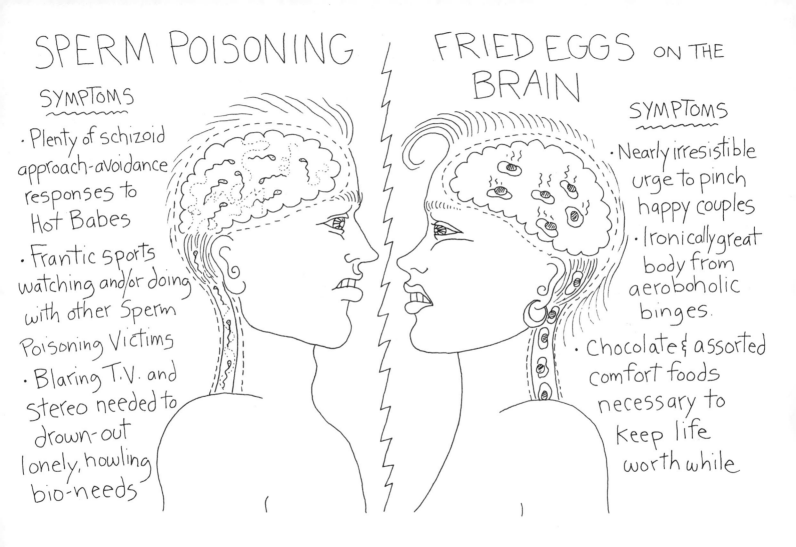

SPERM POISONING

SYMPTOMS

- Plenty of schizoid approach-avoidance responses to Hot Babes
- Frantic sports watching and/or doing with other Sperm Poisoning Victims
- Blaring T.V. and stereo needed to drown-out lonely, howling bio-needs

FRIED EGGS ON THE BRAIN

SYMPTOMS

- Nearly irresistible urge to pinch happy couples
- Ironically great body from aeroboholic binges.
- Chocolate & assorted comfort foods necessary to keep life worth while

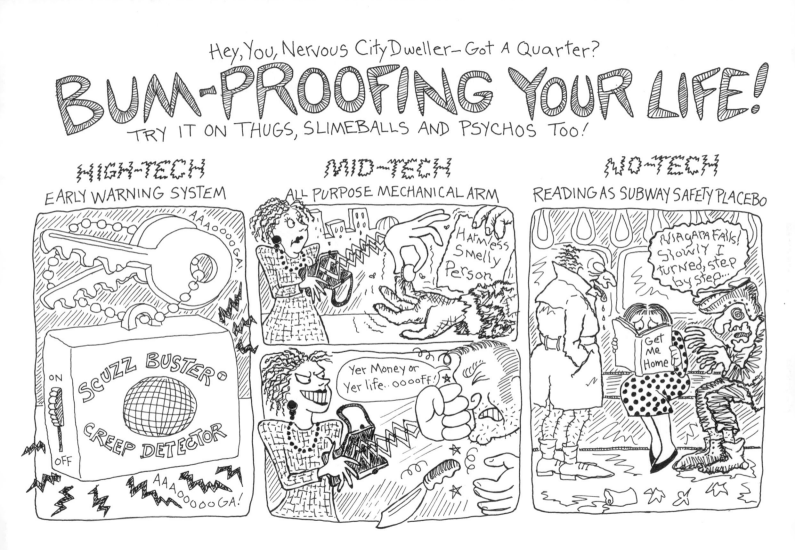

THINK TWICE, CURIOUS GIRLFRIEND, BEFORE YOU TALK YOUR BOYFRIEND INTO TELLING YOU WHAT HE'S THINKING
She's one mighty fine aging Sex Kitten
5x12=60 16x23=368 53x936= 49,608....
She's so cute when she tries to hide her cellulite
I never thought I'd fall in love with a frizzy-haired neurotic with a big butt.
She's smart, but luckily a sucker for compliments
I suppose I should say something romantic. Nothing too good— I don't want her to get big ideas.

THE 1-MINUTE DREAM DATE

ALSO KNOWN IN LOVE WAR LINGO AS "GUERILLA DATING"

IT'S EASY! IT'S FUN! IT'S SNEAKY!

PICK THE HUNKIEST GUY IN YOUR CORPORATE WORK WORLD

You know, the one who reminds you most of the cool boys in high school who didn't know you were alive.

FIND A ROMANTIC SETTING

You'll need a place to stalk your unsuspecting prey. You have the advantage in this relationship since He doesn't even know the two of you are dating.

Wanna piece of Gum?

O.K., Thanks

BREATH of ROMANCE CHEWING GUM

OFFER HIM A REFRESHING STICK OF GUM

As he chews, pretend the two of you are dining in an expensive French restaurant. He insists on paying the check.

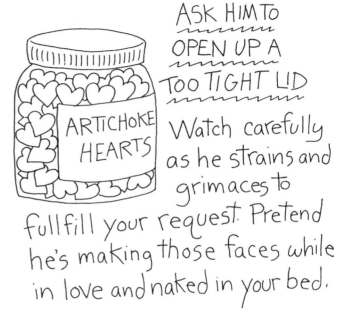

ARTICHOKE HEARTS

ASK HIM TO OPEN UP A TOO TIGHT LID

Watch carefully as he strains and grimaces to fullfill your request. Pretend he's making those faces while in love and naked in your bed.

NOW WAKE UP AND GET BACK TO WORK!

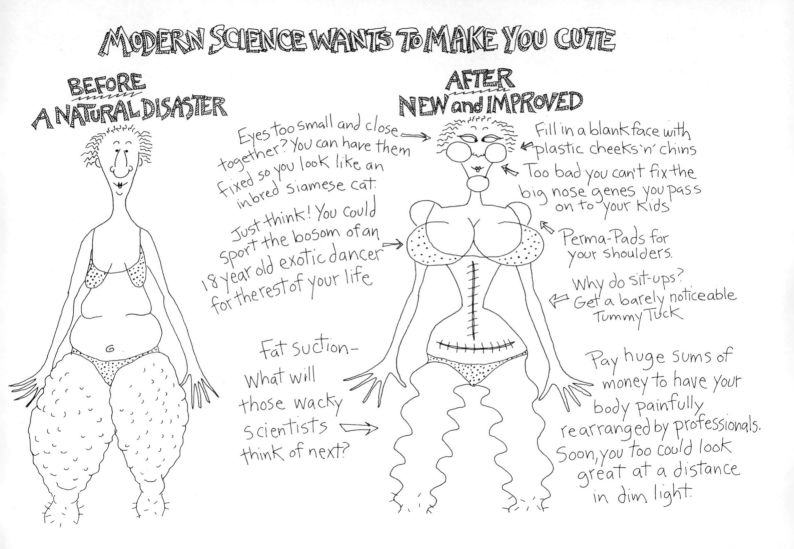

MICRO-NUKE MEAL MASTER
Prepare Romantic Glow-in-the-Dark Dinners
Remove Old Fashioned Nutrients FAST
Special "Quick Fluff" setting for Popcorn and Wet Poodles
Tasty Cakes with Rock-hard centers and Liquid edges—just try doing that in a conventional oven!
MODERN CAKES
YUMMY SPUDS
PIPING HOT ALBINO TURKEY IN AN INSTANT!

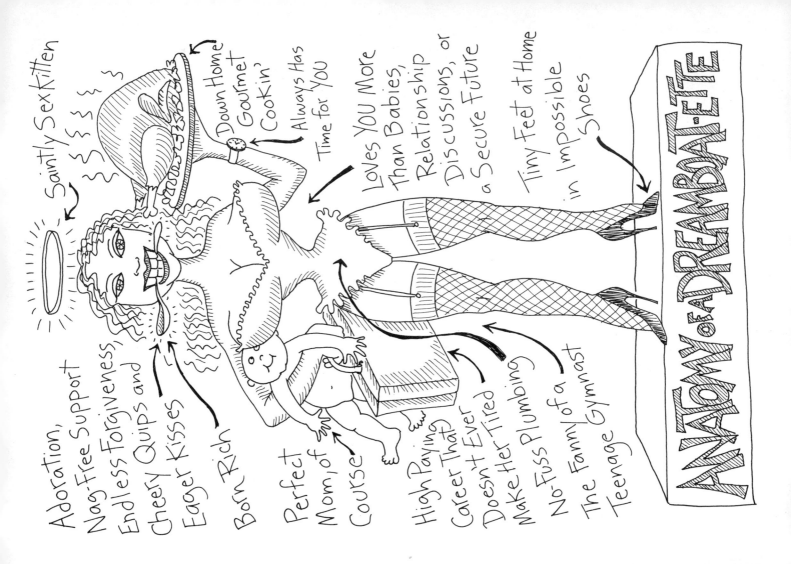

Saintly Sex Kitten

Down Home Gourmet Cookin'

Always Has Time for You

Loves YOU More Than Babies, Relationship Discussions, or a Secure Future

Tiny Feet at Home in Impossible Shoes

Adoration, Nag-Free Support Endless Forgiveness, Cheery Quips and Eager Kisses

Born Rich

Perfect Mom, of Course

High Paying Career That Doesn't Ever Make Her Tired

No-Fuss Plumbing

The Fanny of a Teenage Gymnast

ANATOMY of a DREAMBOAT-ETTE

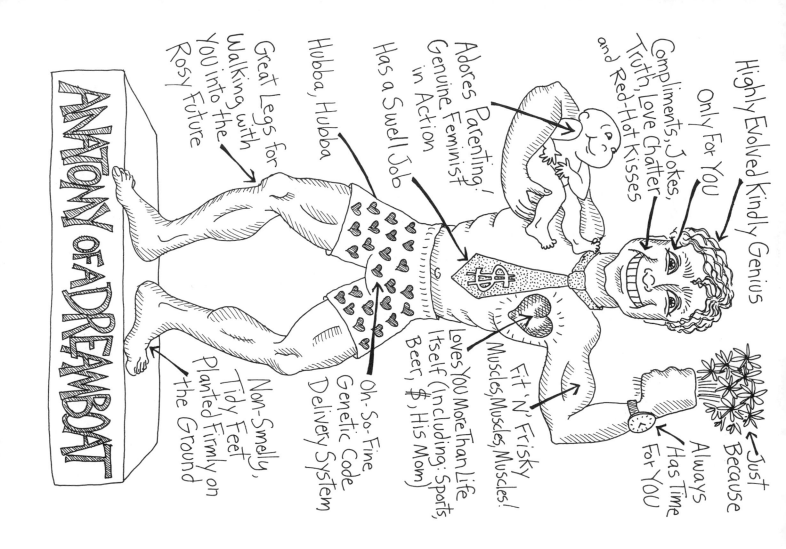

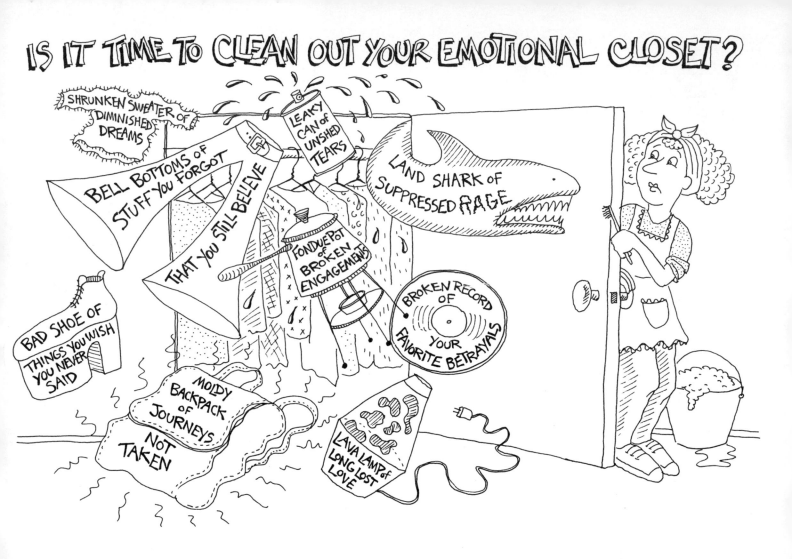

SPECIAL TREATS FROM GOD

ANY TIME YOU EAT CHOCOLATE AND DON'T FEEL GUILTY

REALLY GREAT BAD MOVIES

TAX REFUNDS

15 GREEN LIGHTS IN A ROW

PERFECT COFFEE

COMPLIMENTS THAT YOU KNOW ARE TRUE

HOT SHOWERS WITH GOOD WATER PRESSURE

SHOES THAT LOOK AS GOOD AS THEY FEEL

SATISFYING SNAPPY COMEBACKS TO RUDE INSULTS

CLOTHES THAT MAKE YOU LOOK JUST LIKE YOU WISH YOU DID

ALL YOUR FINGERNAILS ARE PERFECT AT THE SAME TIME

PHONE CALLS FROM NOSEY COMPUTERS

YOUR PET POSSESSED BY SATAN

SPILLED MILK UNDER THE REFRIGERATOR

DRY CLEAN ONLY

TASTELESS CHICKEN AND GRAINY PINK TOMATOES

LONG ENOUGH TO RUIN YOUR BEST BOOTS

TOILET PAPER THAT FOLLOWS YOU AROUND ON YOUR SHOE WHEN YOU'RE NOT LOOKING

BURNT TOAST

THOSE BLACK MASCARA BLOBS THAT GROW IN THE CORNERS OF EYES

PRE-PROM PIMPLES

YOU, A DEPARTMENT STORE DRESSING ROOM, AND A LOAD OF FIGURE-FAULT-ACCENTUATING FASHIONS

TINY TRIALS FROM SATAN

How's your FINANCIAL HEALTH? THE WARNING SIGNS

Surgically enhanced Pertness of Nose and Bosom

Skin Rash if exposed to non-designer less than 100% natural clothing fibers

Addicted to "Her" Colors.

More Money Than Sense

Nails sculpted by hired Foreign Ladies

Chez Yup Nouvelle Power Brunch

20 Angst Points

Run around like a crazy person on a fool's errand for a high-powered fool.

100 Angst Points

Sneeze and accidentally Fart at the same time during a career-critical power meeting.

75 Angst Points

The promotion you were promised goes to the Lecherous Demon-Nerd, making him your New Boss instead.

45 Angst Points

Laugh in the face of Corporate Death! Wear clothes you actually like to the office.

25 Angst Points

Brown Nose a particularly Loathsome Client.

Thousands of cards for all the ways your job tries to ruin your day!

I want Deal-A-Day. I don't care how much it costs. Here's my credit card and a blank check.
Send to:
Chump Relief Industries
Corporate, America

STRANDED on the SEA of LOVE CONFLICTS

BIOLOGICAL CLOCKS V.S. FEAR OF COMMITMENT

SECRET JERK-PRODUCING FEARS
V.S.
SECRET ROMANTIC FANTASIES

T.V. TAINTED BODY IMAGES
V.S.
T.V. TAINTED BODY IMAGES

BAD MOODS V.S. P.M.S.

VULGAR TABLE MANNERS V.S. MINDLESS ATONAL HUMMING

OUTSIDE LOVE INTERESTS V.S. BARELY CONCEALED HOMICIDAL URGES

VICIOUS RAZOR STUBBLE LEGS V.S. SNORING ON PURPOSE

Can you do the "Equality" that new Love Dance craze that's sweeping our generation?
I'll certainly pretend that I do if it will keep me out of trouble. Shall we dance?
Women have changed role models from the "Perky Doormat" to the "Corporate Earth Goddess." The transition is still a little shaky, but how do you like it so far?
Thank goodness you women are still highly vulnerable when it comes to your looks!

The women are right and if you men would just trust us, we'll prove you're all a bunch of jerks.
Ha! We've got 10,000 years of civilization and inertia on our side!
Oh, yeah? Well, we're learning to love and honor our womanly selves and that makes us alot pickier about who we let trash our lives!
Excuse me, but I think I'll go date someone 15 years younger than you now.

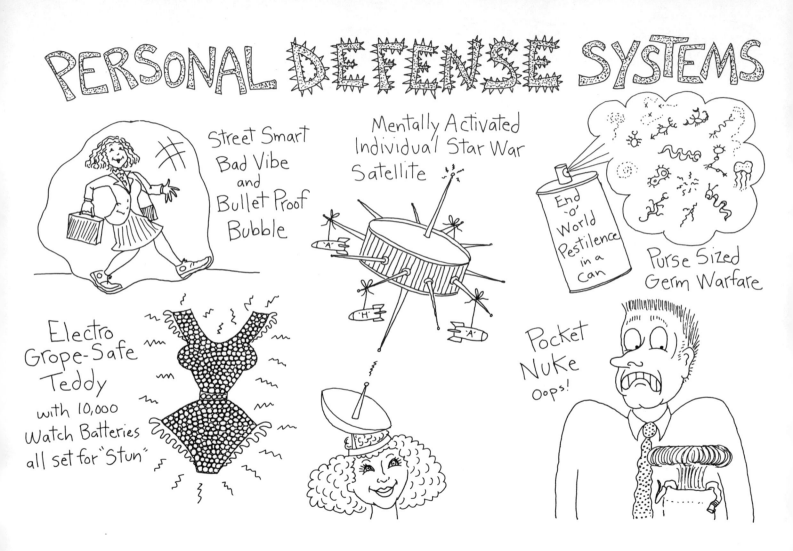

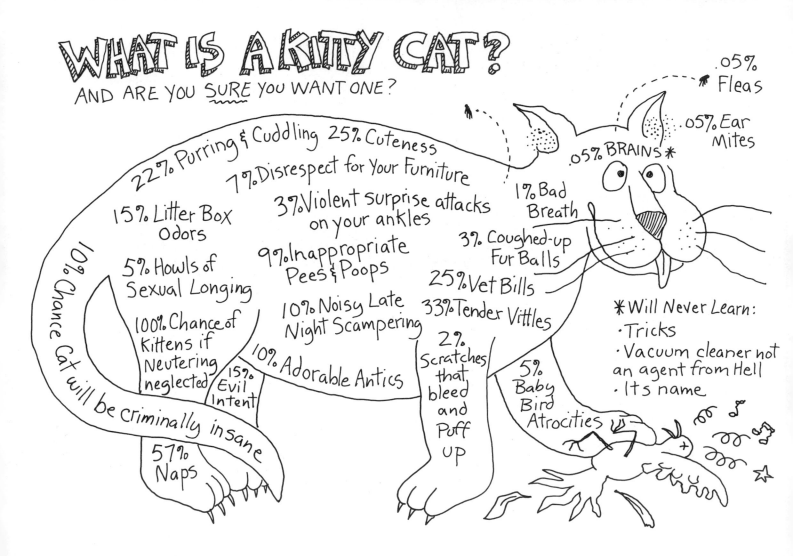

IT'S NOT WHAT YOU THINK YOU KNOW
IT'S WHAT YOU DON'T KNOW YOU THINK!

As a miserable neurotic mess, you should gladly pay big bucks to Psycho Science to find out. Lucky for you, here are FREE SAMPLES of your innermost thoughts—

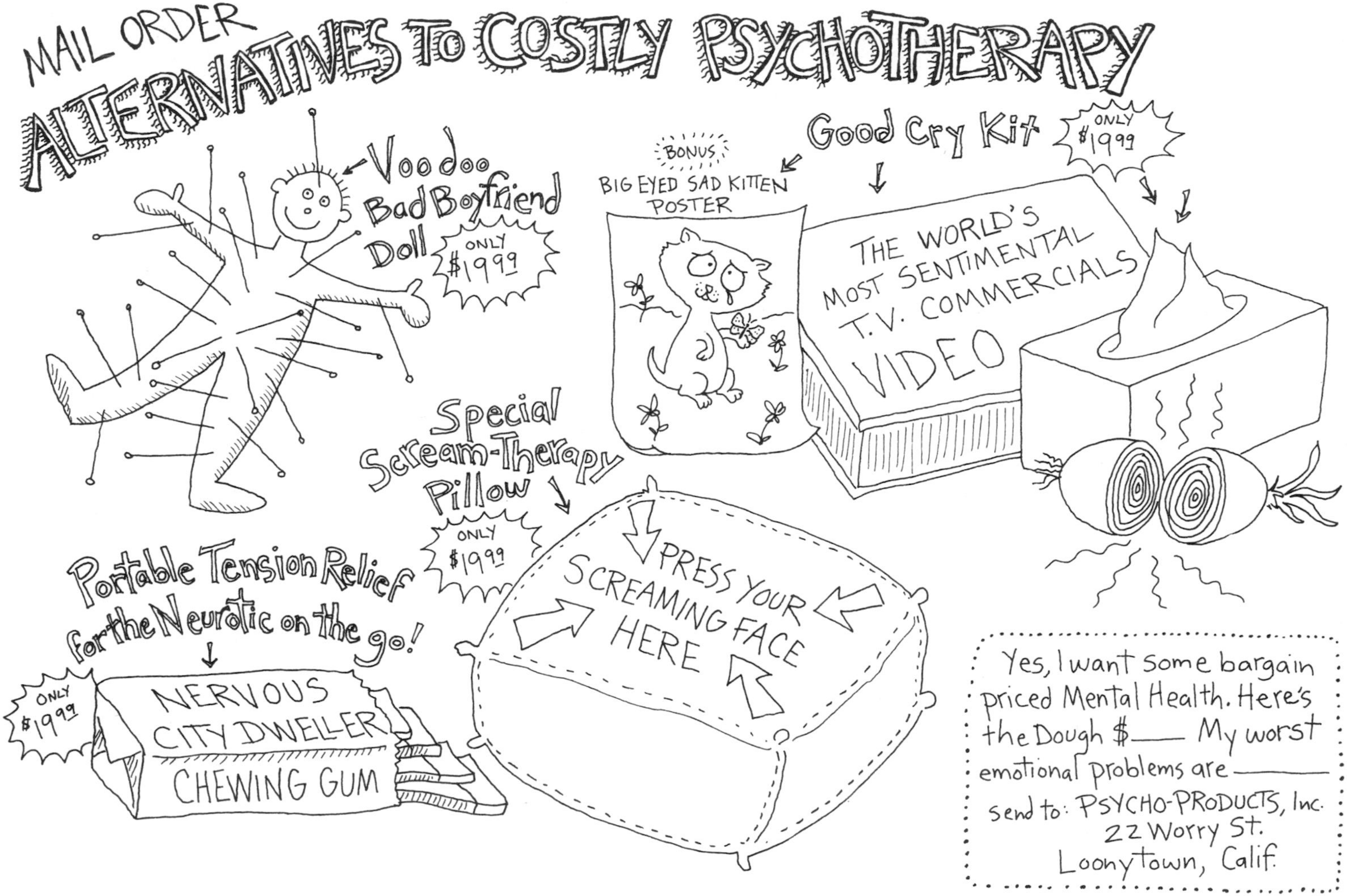
MAIL ORDER
ALTERNATIVES TO COSTLY PSYCHOTHERAPY
Voodoo Bad Boyfriend Doll
ONLY $19.99
Good Cry Kit
ONLY $19.99
BONUS
BIG EYED SAD KITTEN POSTER
THE WORLD'S MOST SENTIMENTAL T.V. COMMERCIALS VIDEO
Special Scream-Therapy Pillow
ONLY $19.99
PRESS YOUR SCREAMING FACE HERE
Portable Tension Relief for the Neurotic on the go!
ONLY $19.99
NERVOUS CITY DWELLER
CHEWING GUM
Yes, I want some bargain priced Mental Health. Here's the Dough $____ My worst emotional problems are ____
send to: PSYCHO-PRODUCTS, Inc.
22 Worry St.
Loonytown, Calif.

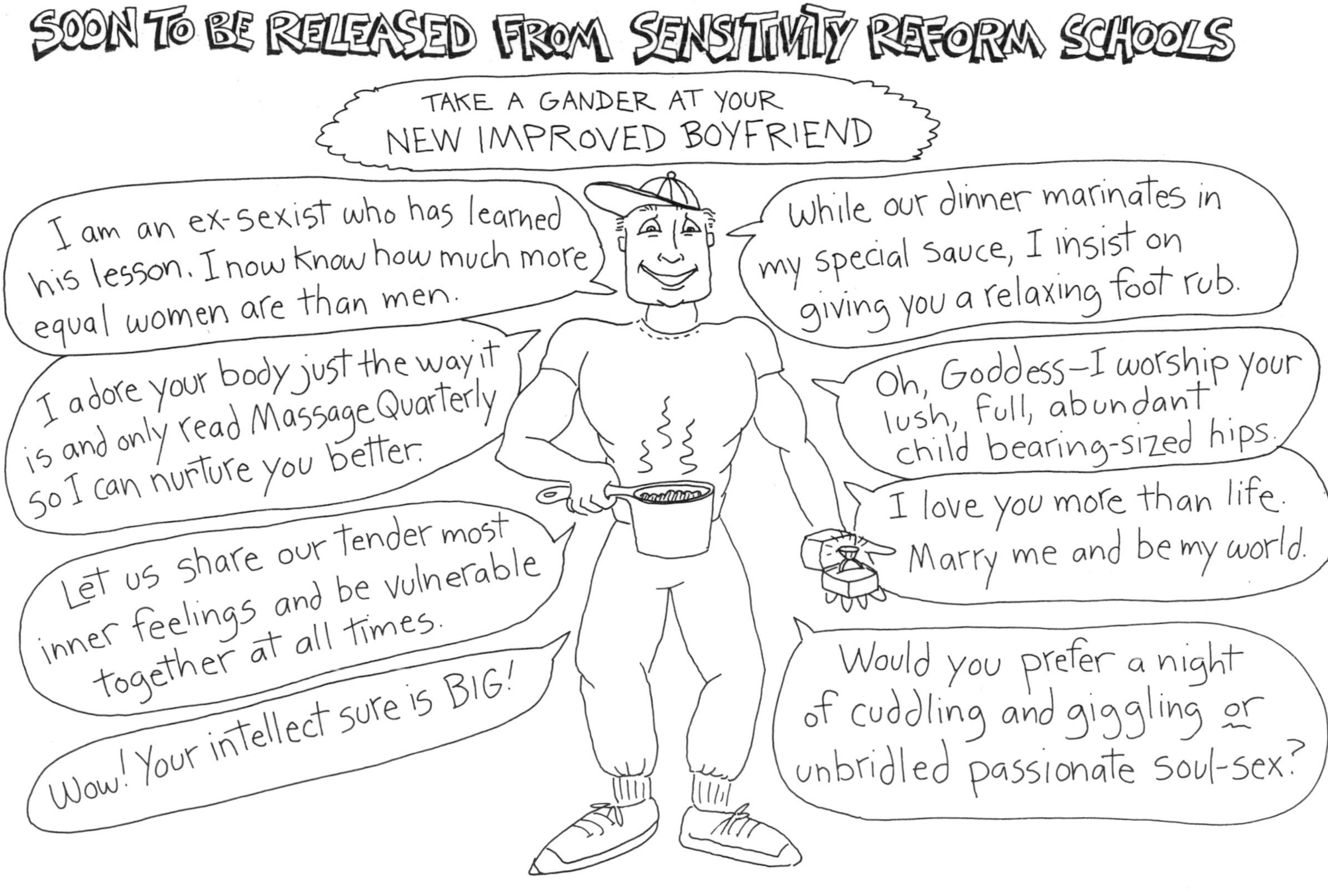
SOON TO BE RELEASED FROM SENSITIVITY REFORM SCHOOLS
TAKE A GANDER AT YOUR NEW IMPROVED BOYFRIEND
I am an ex-sexist who has learned his lesson. I now know how much more equal women are than men.
While our dinner marinates in my special sauce, I insist on giving you a relaxing foot rub.
I adore your body just the way it is and only read Massage Quarterly so I can nurture you better.
Oh, Goddess—I worship your lush, full, abundant child bearing-sized hips.
I love you more than life. Marry me and be my world.
Let us share our tender most inner feelings and be vulnerable together at all times.
Wow! Your intellect sure is BIG!
Would you prefer a night of cuddling and giggling or unbridled passionate soul-sex?

Libby Reid spent her "Wonder Years" in Morgantown, West Virginia. She worked as a Waitress, Cheese Hostess, Glamorous Fashion Model, Radio Announcer and Graphic Art Slave before finding her True Calling as a Cartoonist. Her first book was Do You Hate Your Hips More Than Nuclear War? She now dwells in New York City where she likes to notice stuff.

PHOTO BY GENE BAGNATO